I0601201

Always and Forever

Stephanie Taylor

Clean Reads
www.cleanreads.com

ALWAYS AND FOREVER
Copyright © 2017 STEPHANIE TAYLOR
ISBN 978-1-62135-666-0
Cover Model: Rob Bierman
Cover Art Designed by AM DESIGNS STUDIO

This is a work of fiction. Names, places, characters, and events are fictitious in every regard. Any similarities to actual events and persons, living or dead, are purely coincidental. Any trademarks, service marks, product names, or named features are assumed to be the property of their respective owners, and are used only for reference. There is no implied endorsement if any of these terms are used. Except for review purposes, the reproduction of this book in whole or part, electronically or mechanically, constitutes a copyright violation.

You know who you are...

Chapter One

He was the first thing on her mind in the morning;
the last thing on her mind before she fell asleep…

EVERY MORNING, LIAM'S text came right at 6 am. Rolling over in bed grappling for her phone, Cora tried not to feel the race of excitement that he still thought of her. It was over between them. It had been for six months. Yet he still insisted on texting her, sending her sweet messages that made her heart go *pitter-patter*.

Good morning! I miss you.

Cora didn't respond. She almost never did. But it didn't stop him, nor did it stop her from wishing things were different.

She didn't think either of them had seen their breakup coming. It had been so good, so perfect between them, and then they'd started talking marriage, and she'd balked. She blamed herself. Even when she thought she was ready, when push came to shove, she'd retreated like a turtle into its shell.

Before dating Liam, she'd been married for fifteen years. It was a hard adjustment to be alone, but she had finally settled in a place where she was happy. Then the gauntlet had been thrown and threatened to change every-thing again.

After a year of dating Liam, she had still been hesi-tant to pull the trigger on moving forward. They'd talked about getting engaged plenty of times. They both had clearly wanted the next step, but as usual, the fear had crept in. Cora chalked it up to her being nine years older and wondering if Liam was really prepared for a ready-made family and all it entailed. He was great with her three kids, and they loved him, but dating was a far cry from actually being a live-in father.

Then the fight had happened. They'd hurled angry words at each other, frustration eating them alive and manifesting into a creature neither of them could control. Why couldn't he be happy keeping things the way they were for another year or more? What was the rush?

It had been both an insult and a relief to watch him leave after their argument. Her kids were finally forging a better relationship with their father, and they needed to be her focus. Sam, her ex-husband, could be flaky. If he met someone again and decided to pull another disap-pearing act, she had to be there to pick up the pieces. She couldn't do that when Liam consumed her.

He'd come back to talk to her later, but Cora had de-cided during his absence it wouldn't work. Not a single word from him in over two weeks. It had stung. Still did. For someone who claimed to love her, his pride sure stood tall and immovable.

They were in two different stages of life. He was still young, having fun with friends every weekend. She wanted someone to hold her at night while they watched a movie and focus on growing old together. Since she was halfway there, it seemed time was of the essence. Time certainly wasn't doing her any favors these days, but marriage didn't *have* to be part of the equation.

Forcing herself out of bed, Cora trudged into the

bathroom to shower, her thoughts never far from Liam. Every morning started out this way, analyzing, wondering... wishing things were different but knowing they couldn't be.

In a rare moment of self-pity, she allowed a lone tear to escape. He hadn't fought for her, only with her. Too easily, one by one the men in her life had dismissed her. She'd wrestled to keep her head above water, but she was slowly drowning in an ocean of self-doubt. What was wrong with her? Why did it have to be everything or nothing?

After her shower, she wiped away a circle of steam in her mirror with her towel. The woman staring back at her wasn't any different than she had been two years ago when she and Liam had first begun their story. Still the same grayish-blue eyes, dark hair, and wrinkles. Liam used to get so mad when she complained about her age.

How could she not be self-conscious when a man ten years her junior was still in his prime, attractive, and determined to date her?

Cora's shoulders sagged.

With a deep breath, Cora jutted her chin out and squared her shoulders. She wouldn't let anything get her down. She wouldn't let any man push her, certainly not Liam. It was in these moments she tried to convince herself he'd never really cared how she felt about the situation – for her sanity, for her future, for her healing heart. It had just been something of a novelty for an older woman to show interest. Maybe she was one of his weekend conquests that just stuck a little longer than most. Maybe he'd just wanted something he thought he couldn't have.

Her shoulders drooped again. She was a fool. Cora knew he still cared, probably even still loved her, otherwise he wouldn't text. If she hadn't shut him down so completely when he'd come to her house with a hopeful gleam in his eyes, they might have had a chance. Bottom line, she had gotten spooked… again. It shamed her, but at the time she'd seen no other option but to send him on his way. After so many years with Sam, she wasn't sure she was ready to commit to someone again after only a year.

Liam had given her no indication or warning signs she should worry. Looking back on her relationship with Sam, there had been plenty of warning signs. Hindsight was always clear. So what couldn't she see with Liam? Was his worst offense wanting to be with her?

After getting dressed for the day, Cora woke up the kids to get ready for school. She cooked breakfast, her eyes bleary and tired. She needed coffee.

Jolie, her sixteen year old, came down first. She'd discovered makeup and curling irons. It hurt Cora's heart to see her growing up so fast. "Morning, Mom." Her usual cheery self, Jolie gave her a tight hug and kissed her cheek.

"Good morning, beautiful!" Time for Cora's everything-is-great face. Jolie was entirely too perceptive otherwise, and Cora just didn't feel like explaining why, almost exactly one year after their breakup, she was still sad Liam wasn't around.

"Bacon!" Ashton cried from mid-way down the stairs. Aldin wasn't far behind.

"Of course!" she called with a grin. Her twin boys loved food. At eleven, they were starting to fill out and looked like tiny men. She loved how their blue eyes were full of playful mischief.

Eating breakfast was always family time, as was dinner. They all sat down together and filled their stomachs with bacon, oatmeal and fruit. Cora didn't believe in letting them start a school day hungry.

Soon enough, they finished their plates and put them in the dishwasher. Returning to their chair, they slung their backpacks off the floor and onto their backs. It was Friday, and they were ready to get the day over and start their weekend.

While Jolie stood next to the door waiting for the bus, Cora smiled. She'd blinked, and they were older, wiser, and closer to adulthood. The telltale grumble of the bus signaled them to walk out the door. She gave the twins a quick hug and kiss, thankful they still allowed it – for now. Jolie opened her arms before Cora was done with the twins.

Cora went into her embrace without a second thought. When she pulled back, Cora smoothed her cheek and tucked a stray piece of hair behind her ear. "You're beautiful. Inside and out."

Jolie gave her an award-winning smile. "I love you, Mom."

She watched as her children filed onto the bus, a smile tugging at her lips.

This was what life was really about.

ONCE AGAIN, SHE hadn't responded to his text. Liam tried hard not to let the fact get him down. He knew she received them. Occasionally he'd see the telltale three dots that she was typing…but only rarely did anything ever come through.

He missed her. Had missed her since she'd sent him packing. Sometimes it manifested as a physical ache. Cora had completed him in ways he'd never realized until she was gone. Since then, he'd spent his weekends trying to forget her, hanging out with friends, flirting with cookie-cutter blondes looking for an eight-second ride in the bar bathroom.

None of them were Cora.

But the next morning, she was always the first thing on his mind. No amount of women or alcohol or time away could exorcise her from his mind. So he'd continued to text her for months now, hoping against hope she'd see he still cared and somehow he'd be at the forefront of her mind, too. Hoping she'd be ready to move on.

Yes, she'd freaked when he told her he wanted to marry her. Still did. He doubted if he could live up to Cora's expectations, but he'd certainly try. And he certainly didn't want to be the second man in her kids' life to fail them. But he couldn't be anything to them if Cora wouldn't let him.

He should've known better than to leave Cora after the argument, but they had both been so heated, he feared saying something he'd regret. They'd spent a year together, falling more and more in love, and all she'd asked for was a little more time. But how much time did she need? She either wanted to marry him or she didn't. After those two weeks, he'd come back with a ring in his pocket and ready to beg her for forgiveness. Not exactly how he'd envisioned a proposal, but when she saw how serious he was, would she understand his sincerity?

Ultimately, though, she'd been the one to call it off. He never even got the opportunity to beg. The second his foot hit the gravel drive, he'd looked up to see her standing on her porch, resignation written all over her face.

Cora was painfully insecure, but telling him she wasn't ready to get married felt an awful lot like rejection. It had taken him a long while to convince her their age difference wasn't a big deal. For a long time, it was never even mentioned. And then they'd argued and the wall had been erected before he could take back his words. He'd failed her and failed himself by letting his anger get the best of him.

He'd taken a second to doubt, a second to question his own ability to provide everything a family would need. But was anyone truly an expert? Didn't they learn along the way? He'd thought about how being married would affect the kids relationship with their father. If Cora could handle a lifetime with a man almost ten years younger and all that entailed. It was no easy task moving in and becoming a father right away. They'd done so well for so long… He wasn't sure he'd ever fully understand how it had happened. All he knew was they'd both hesitated and Cora jumped on the break up wagon and never looked back. A perfect storm, he supposed.

It made him wonder if she had ever truly been happy.

Liam wouldn't give up until she looked into his eyes and told him to. You didn't fall in love with someone the way he did with Cora and just walk away counting your losses. He'd given her time, probably too much of it. But he would fight for what was real and good and right. Cora was all of those things and so much more.

As Liam went through his morning routine, he once again came up blank with how to deal with Cora. If he tried to push his way back into her life, he'd be met with resistance of epic proportions. In a fight or flight situation, Cora was always a flight. She'd been hurt enough in her lifetime it wasn't worth it to her to get hurt again. He admitted it was his fault for walking away and not giving her the confidence she needed in their relationship to move forward. But it had been *one* moment, one argument, amongst a year of breathtaking memories.

If he let it, he knew he'd get angry and resentful. Human nature was a jerk that way. Instead, he channeled his energy into working his ranch and making a few phone calls during his lunch break.

It wasn't until that evening, when he sat down at a lonely table with a frostbitten tray of tasteless food that he allowed himself to think about her again.

Six months had passed. Six months of texting her every morning. Six months of wondering if she would thaw enough to talk. He just couldn't believe it was really over. Couldn't accept it.

He'd thought if he gave her some space she'd work through her demons and come back to him. But the months were ticking away, and he was pretty sure if he didn't do something now, her walls would be fully constructed and bulletproof before too much longer. He'd broken through them once before; he could do it again. It wasn't a job for the weak, and it certainly wasn't a job he could accomplish if he wasn't all in.

And, of course, he was *all* in.

Chapter Two

Life hurts a lot more than death...

THE BALMY SPRING air rustled Cora's hair as she used her foot to rock the porch swing back and forth. A year ago, she'd be sitting here waiting for Liam's truck to come down her gravel drive around now. Tonight, it remained silent and empty. The moon was slowly making its ascent through the sky, and the first stars were beginning to pop. Cora had a childish tradition of wishing on the first one she saw, even if she knew it was silly.

She remembered the evening she'd taught her kids to wish on a star, and she smiled. She didn't even know if the twins remembered it, but every so often, she caught Jolie looking up at the stars quietly, focused on only one.

So lost in the memory, Cora smiled when her mind conjured the familiar truck coming down the drive, kicking up dust in its wake. It wasn't until she snapped out of her daze that she realized he was actually here. She thought about escaping inside, but she'd look childish. Her heart was beating a wild rhythm in her chest at the thought of seeing Liam again. She rubbed her eyes just to make sure they weren't playing tricks on her. But if her eyes were, her ears were too because they heard the telltale crunch of gravel.

Cora took a deep breath and let it out slowly.

When the creaky car door opened and Liam's dusty boots rested on her driveway, she closed her eyes for a moment fighting against the urge to run to him and kiss him senseless.

He donned his black cowboy hat as his eyes met hers, and he closed the truck door. He wore a black and red plaid button up. His jeans rode low on his hips, hugging him in all the right places the way she longed to. She tried to look away but couldn't. Such beauty deserved to be savored.

"Evenin'," he drawled in a familiar low timbre, tipping his hat.

Cora's throat went dry, and she found she couldn't respond. She gave him a wan smile instead.

He ambled toward the steps, taking his time, no doubt, just to drive her insane. She needed him to say what he came to say and then leave. Her heart couldn't take the sight of him. She'd invested so much time and hope in their future together and to see him so gorgeous, so virile before her left her wanting to kick him in the shins.

"How have you been?" Liam spoke first.

She could tell by the way he fiddled with the back pockets of his jeans he was uneasy. Funny how she could still read him some six months after last seeing him.

All Cora could do was nod her answer.

"Can I come up?" He eyed her from the bottom of the porch steps but waited.

Still not sure she could speak, she nodded again and slid over in the swing. The swing they'd sat on every evening after the kids went to bed and made out like horny teenagers. The swing where the argument had taken place and brought their relationship to a screeching halt.

When his weight settled next to her, thighs brushing, she moved a little further away.

"I won't bite," he said through a tight grin.

Finally she found her voice. "Why are you here?"

Liam huffed out a deep breath and looked out to the front of the house, thinking. "Well, for starters, I wanted to see how you were doing. I haven't heard from you in a while. You haven't answered my texts lately."

"I'm fine." Cora crossed her arms over her chest, feeling self-conscious in his presence. She hadn't been expecting him and wasn't wearing a lick of makeup, nor had she brushed her hair since this morning. Despite everything, she still wanted to look good in front of him.

"Why *don't* you answer my texts?" he finally asked quietly.

"I don't have anything to say." Oh, but she did. But once she did that, Niagara Falls would have a hard time keeping up.

They sat in silence for a long moment, the swing creaking under their weight as it moved back and forth.

"I've missed you." His words were so soft, she thought maybe she imagined them.

Cora swallowed thickly and clenched her eyes closed. "Don't," she warned.

"Why? I've texted you every morning for six months. I've been patient. Everything is so screwed up, but you didn't even give me a chance to explain."

"The longer the explanation, the bigger the lie," she threw at him, avoiding eye contact. She knew once she looked into his green eyes, she'd be lost all over again.

"And an explanation of cause is not a justification by reason." His voice was calm. Too calm. Too sexy. Too close.

"I can't do this." She shot to her feet only for Liam to catch her wrist and drag her back down beside him.

He continued talking like he hadn't just manhandled her. "I didn't let you know I was coming because I was afraid you wouldn't answer the door."

"How very astute of you."

"I just… needed to see you again, Cor. I didn't think it would take this long for you to figure everything out."

"I figured everything out the night you left."

His eyes clenched closed. When he opened them again, they were pleading. "I miss you. I just needed to see you."

"And now you have. You can see yourself out the way you came in."

She tried to stand again, but his fingers threaded through hers and held fast. For a moment, she struggled to remove her hand from his, but he didn't even act like her struggle fazed him.

"Don't you remember how good it is between us? Nights just like this doing nothing but holding each other and kissing?"

Cora sneered but said nothing. Didn't he know a true relationship had nothing to do with kissing and everything about sticking around, even when things got difficult? She'd already had enough people check out on her.

"There's more to a relationship than holding and kissing each other," she murmured, still trying to extricate her hand.

"I agree. I also remember spending some quality time with your kids and falling in love with them just as much as I did you. Going bowling together, dinner together, laughing together."

Finally her hand was free, and Liam sighed dramatically. His arm outstretched behind her on the swing.

Cora shot to her feet and paced for a few moments before whirling to face him again. "You said you weren't like Sam. You made me believe you wouldn't leave."

"I didn't leave, Cora! We had an argument. *You* said you weren't ready. I know that wasn't code for breaking up; it was just you trying to figure out what comes next. If I was what your kids needed; what *you* needed. I never thought we'd both let this much time pass."

"You got spooked. Things were getting too serious, and you ran." She sounded like a petulant child, but it was how she felt.

Liam bulleted to his feet and approached her, his dark gaze in direct contrast to his casual body language. "You thought you already had it all figured out by the time I came back, didn't you? You thought I *was* like Sam. I'm scared, too. If I wasn't, I wouldn't be human. You and those kids are *everything* I've ever wanted in life and it scares me to death. The last thing I ever meant to do was hurt you. Or them. But you ran, too. You got scared because I mentioned the "M" word, and it was easier for you to just call it quits before risking getting hurt. I gave *you* plenty of time after I told you I wanted to date you to figure out what you wanted."

Cora swallowed against the lump in her throat but said nothing as she leaned against the porch railing.

He stepped closer and closer to her. "I miss you, Cora. I want this. I want you. I want the kids."

By then, big tears were forming, but she refused to let them fall. She thought of all the moments he'd broken down her defenses. All the times she'd believed in their love. "Two people have to be willing to try again. And I'm not willing. I don't want to get married again."

Liam studied her, his green eyes swirling with regret and determination. His hand came up and touched her jaw, his thumb tracing the bone. Their eyes met and Cora inhaled the scent that was uniquely his.

He was going to kiss her. She'd kissed him too many times not to know what those smoldering eyes meant. Her head screamed for her to move away, to protect herself against more pain, but her heart softly called to him, beckoning him home.

Trapped in an emotional tug-of-war, she didn't move nor did she respond when his mouth softly settled on hers. He worked against her clenched lips with a few delicious tugs until he pulled back and smiled.

"Open for me, Cora." He dipped his mouth against hers again, his tongue tracing the seam of her lips.

Her knees went weak. Her heart pounded. But she couldn't give in. She just couldn't. She had her children to think about, and they couldn't withstand Liam leaving them again.

She couldn't withstand it.

"Let me in," he whispered, his breath hot on her face. His body was flush with hers now, his steely strength a reminder of how wonderful it felt to be in his arms.

Quick tufts of air left her nose. Their eyes locked, and she knew without a doubt it was a mistake to get caught up in those green eyes again. He'd broken her, shattered her heart into a million pieces. Looking at him now, she wanted to give in. Her willpower when it came to Liam was the equivalent of a kid being handed a cookie and told not to eat it.

Not for the first time, she wondered if maybe she had been too quick to write him off. It was just an argument. He really had given her all the space she'd needed when they first started dating, and backed off when their age difference got to be too much. But when she realized it was Liam she wanted, he'd accepted her with eager, open arms.

So why was she fighting him so hard? It was just an argument. Was the age gap still the problem? Cora didn't think she'd ever be fully okay with it, but for right now, that didn't seem to be her biggest issue.

So what was it?

Once again, Liam's kiss whispered against her mouth. He knew exactly what he was doing to her, the devil. His devious grin as he continued to tease her reminded her how much he loved a good chase.

Just as she was about to succumb to his advances, she remembered the agony of watching him leave. Pain coursed through her like a stinging bee.

Wrenching away from him, she used her anger to fuel her words.

"We're over." She crossed her arms over her breasts and looked out away from him, unable to stand the closeness. "You need to leave."

"I'm not leaving, Cor. I'm here to stay. You made me leave before, but we're right back here again. You can pretend to hate me all you want. I broke through your walls once; I'll do it again."

"You seem to be awful sure of yourself."

Liam's hand came to rest above her head as he casually leaned down, his eyes smiling into hers. "You don't have the kind of relationship we had and just give up."

"Funny you waited six months to figure that out."

His eyes narrowed. "I've texted you every morning since *we* argued. It didn't take me six months to figure anything out except that you're a chicken, Cora. Sam messed with you; I get that. You have daddy issues; I get that too. But that's been over for years. You can't use it as an excuse forever. Eventually, you'll need to answer for your decisions."

Cora was so angry her hands shook as she walked to her front door. She hated the fact she only walked passed him because he allowed it. He controlled his hulking strength, even when angry, and she was always aware of that.

Slowly, she lifted a shaking finger and pointed it at him accusingly. Her eyes filled with tears. "*You* left. Not me. I watched you. And it broke everything inside of me."

The second Liam registered her tears, his face softened, and he took a step toward her. She held her hands up to stop his advance.

Bouncing headlights coming down her drive distracted them both as they squinted into the light. Cora recognized the blue lights on top and foreboding settled under her skin.

The sight of the two uniformed policemen walking toward her would have alarmed her if she hadn't had her whole world in the house behind her. She wondered if Ashton and Aldin had gotten into some mischief.

"Good evenin', ma'am," the one on the left said. "Are you Cora?"

Cora narrowed her eyes. "Yes, I am."

"I'm Officer Keene and this is Officer Caplin. Could we come in for a few minutes? We have some unfortunate news to deliver."

Cora opened the door and stepped aside as Liam stood behind her, his curiosity palpable. She wasn't sure what was going on. Maybe they had the wrong Cora? How many Coras were in their small town?

"Would you like something to drink?" she finally asked the officers, remembering her manners as she closed the front door. It was then she realized Liam hadn't left and was instead settling in on her sofa like he belonged.

"No," they both said in unison.

"May we sit?" Officer Keene motioned to the couch.

"Could you sit down as well, ma'am?"

Unease flared through Cora. What on earth was going on?

Cora eased down next to Liam and his hand on the small of her back immediately soothed her nerves.

"It's my understanding you're the wife of Sam Easton. Correct?"

"Ex. Ex-wife." Her voice shook despite her false bravado.

"Tonight, at approximately eighteen hundred hours, your ex-husband was involved in a fatal car collision caused by a drunk driver. After looking into all his personal effects, you were listed as his emergency contact. We're sorry for your loss."

For a second, the words didn't compute. "Sam's dead? No, Sam just picked up the kids last weekend for a long lunch down at the lake."

Tears choked her. The kids. The kids had lost their father. She'd mourned him a long time ago, long before he'd died, but that didn't mean she didn't hurt for her children. He had just come back into their lives.

Cora swallowed viciously as the officers stood, donning their hats and headed for the door. Liam stood and ushered them to the door, thanking them for their visit. She just sat there, stunned into silence and disbelief.

Liam's weight settled next to hers again, and his arm wrapped around her shoulder, pulling her to his chest. She was too distracted to pull away. "I'm sorry," he whispered.

"Tell me I'm dreaming. How am I supposed to tell the kids they've lost their father? How am I supposed to tell them he's never coming back?" Tears flowed down her cheeks, and she snatched them away angrily.

"What?" Jolie cried from the hallway behind them.

Cora jumped up, rushing to her. "Honey, come sit down."

"No, tell me what's going on." Jolie's face shone with suspicion.

"Your father… your father was in an accident tonight."

Jolie's eyes searched Cora's for the answer to the unspoken question. When Cora shook her head, Jolie's face crumpled into a child-like cry. She pulled Cora into a fierce hug.

"No," Jolie wailed.

Liam kept his distance, and Cora was grateful. She wasn't sure why he was still here. A part of her wanted to forget everything and ask him for one of his amazing hugs. The other part wanted to kick him out so she could lick her wounds.

Jolie and Cora sat down on the couch together, and Jolie rested her head in Cora's lap. She played with her hair, just like she had when she was a toddler. Ashton and Aldin entered the room then, cautiously.

"Sit down, boys," Liam called. The twins looked at him in curiosity, clearly confused. They hadn't seen Liam in six months, and Jolie was still sobbing.

"What's going on? Why are *you* here? What happened?" Aldin asked Liam.

"There's been an accident," Liam began as Jolie's sobs got louder.

Cora wouldn't admit it, but she was glad Liam was here, yet she couldn't allow him to tell the kids the news.

Stepping in front of him and casting him a pointed look over her shoulder, she said quietly, "Earlier tonight, your father was killed in a car wreck."

Chapter Three

A relationship isn't a big thing, it's a million little things...

THE LIVING ROOM was so silent a pin drop would've echoed through the hall. Everyone, save Jolie who had ran to her room, sat in the quiet; no one even dared to breathe. The twins showed no sign of real emotion, as if they were waiting for the punch line. That worried Cora.

Across the room, Liam was the only one who wasn't devastated at the news Cora's ex-husband had been killed in a car crash. Of course, Liam hadn't given fifteen years of his life to Sam either. Liam didn't understand that despite how her and the kids felt about Sam, he was a part of them, even her.

Liam stood in the doorway, arms crossed, watching her and the boys with his piercing green eyes clearly trying to get a feel for the situation. The twins were old enough at eleven to understand, but it didn't seem to have hit them yet. Shock most likely.

In the meantime, hot tears burned her eyes. She collapsed on the nearest chair and allowed her tears to fall. The kids had just started to adjust to Sam being back in their lives. Sam had started picking Jolie up for regular visits again, and she was finally thriving.

Liam ambled over and ran his palms over her arms and sank his fingers into her shoulder muscles, rubbing gently. He kissed her temple and sighed. "What can I do?"

Cora shook her head, ignoring the fact he wasn't supposed to be here, and another tear finally escaped down her cheeks. She reached back and squeezed his wrist in a minute gesture of thanks. "Nothing. I don't know what to do. Jolie is going to need therapy. Maybe the twins…"

"I might not have liked him, but I sure hate this happened."

"I know. The kids need their father."

His arms came around her shoulders. He gently pulled her against him and squeezed. "I'm here for them. For you. They will always be my first priority."

Cora stiffened. "Now isn't the time for that kind of talk… But thank you for staying," Cora whispered. He always seemed to come along and pick up the pieces when she least expected it.

"I love you," he said against her temple. Then he placed a gentle kiss there.

Cora said nothing but savored the feeling of his protection.

Across the room, Cora looked up and saw Ashton yawning and his eyes drooping. It was getting late and past their bedtime. It would probably be best for them to sleep in if they could tomorrow.

With no immediate surviving family members other than the children, the task of planning her ex-husband's funeral would be daunting. She'd never planned anyone's funeral. Ever.

Wiping away her tears, she stood with Liam by her side.

"Ashton, Aldin, let's get ready for bed. It's getting late." Cora sighed.

The boys stood slowly and ambled up the stairs.

Liam's hand rested on her shoulders. "I got it. You go on. I'll join you in just a bit."

"No, this is something I have to do," she said, resisting his help even though she'd love a few moments to gather her thoughts.

After tucking in the still-stoic twins and making sure Jolie was okay through her locked door, she walked back downstairs into her bedroom. Cora didn't even take the time to see if Liam had left. Right now she had to formulate a plan for what needed to be done. There were so many things to think about. She'd have to handle his estate, find his will, go through his things. Just the thought of having to deal with all that caused her stomach to turn. She sank down to the floor at the foot of her bed and rested her arms on her knees. Gut-wrenching sobs wracked her body.

Cora wept for the man she fell in love with so many years ago. She wept for the man who had given her a doe-eyed daughter and mischievous twin boys. She cried for the marriage that fell in shambles through verbal abuse until she couldn't allow her children to see any more hatred burning in his suddenly empty eyes. Cora wept for the man who'd seemed so adrift when his once perfect family slipped from his grasp. She wept for the man who had fought his way back to his children and made them smile again.

She wasn't sure how long she sat there, wondering about the odd turn her life had taken when Liam's reassuring presence settled next to her, his long legs stretching out and his cowboy boots crossed at the ankles. Cora didn't hesitate to go into his open arms. Having Liam there tonight was providential. He always saved her, showing her the path out of sticky situations where she couldn't see the way.

"I'm not crying because I still love him, you know," she sniveled, unsure why she felt the need to explain. His button-up shirt was raspy against her cheek, but the warmth from his chest seeped into her bones, relaxing her a bit.

His low chuckle vibrated against her arm as his fingertips rubbed a soothing circle on her shoulder.

Cora pushed up to look into his twinkling green eyes. "I mean, I do still love him. I'm not trying to speak ill of the dead. I was married to the man for fifteen years. There will always be a part of me that loves him."

His eyes traveled her face, taking in every detail, every inch. His fingertips traced her jaw and then swept up, and pushing her wet hair from her cheeks. His touch was as soft as a butterfly's wings. "No explanation needed. I understand."

His kindness knocked the wind out of her and her eyes welled with tears again. "Thank you. Thank you for being here. For understanding. For… being here." She let out a weak laugh. Liam kissed her forehead and pushed to his feet. He held his hands out, and she slipped her palms into his. Gently lifting her to her feet, he pulled her straight into a fierce, full body hug.

It made Cora cry all over again. Thoughts, millions of them disseminated through her mind, and she couldn't make sense of them all. Except one. One was prominent. One stood out above all the rest.

Leaning back, she looked into the most beautiful pair of green eyes she'd ever seen. Vibrant, always dancing with boyish joy. Even now, despite their troubles, she could see remnants of a smile in his eyes.

"Do you think he would have done things differently if he knew last night was his last night on earth?"

Liam seemed to ponder her question. "I didn't know him well, and what I did know I didn't like. So I can't really speak for him."

Cora frowned and moved to across the room, thinking about the question herself. Would he have spent the evening with the kids? Apologized for the pain he'd caused her?

After a few seconds, Liam hands at her shoulders urged her to face him again. His fingers came up to her temples and massaged gingerly. How he knew she had the beginnings of a headache were beyond her. When he was done there, he speared his hands through her hair and scratched her scalp. Her eyes slid closed and a soft moan escaped her parted lips. She couldn't help but let her head fall back. He knew just how to make her relax.

Liam's voice was a low rumble next to her ear, whisper soft, like water flowing over stones. "I can't tell you what he would do. I can only tell you what I'd do."

His lips touched her throat as he continued. "I'd start by doing this." A work-roughened hand cradled the back of her neck. He took the time to lavish the pounding pulse at the base of her neck. Her arms wrapped around his waist and drew him closer. The cologne he wore filled her senses, reminding her of sex.

His full lips slid along her jaw and then up to her temples. Then, he placed one sweet kiss on each of her eyelids. "Then I'd do this." Liam's palm slid down her spine and cupped her butt cheeks, pulling her tight against him. She could feel every inch of him. She loved how his eyes darkened to evergreen when he was aroused.

He slid his warm hand underneath the hem of her shirt and smoothed her skin, inhaling her deeply. Cora readied for his kiss. Since the day she'd given in to his advances, he'd taken every opportunity to make her realize their compatibility.

Liam didn't disappoint. His lips touched hers softly yet firmly, and he wasted no time delving deeply, erasing the events of the night from her mind and putting her focus firmly in the present. For just a moment, she forgot the agony her children were facing without their father. She forgot everything except Liam, right here, right now.

When they fell together on the bed, Liam slowed his kisses to a delicious crawl, pinning her hands above her head so their bodies were aligned in all the right places. She wanted him in every way a woman needed a man, and tonight she needed him more than she could ever remember.

Liam pulled away to look at her, a frown etched on his brow, then lowered his forehead to hers. "Sorry. That was inappropriate. I've missed you so much, Cor, and I want to take all your pain away."

He was right to stop. The last thing she needed was to regret a spur of the moment decision. They hadn't worked through anything yet. "Hold me then?" Her voice was sure, much surer than her heart was.

Liam didn't even respond. Instead, he moved to the headboard and pulled her into his warm, opened arms. He sighed when she settled against him, looping one leg over his. His hands explored her shoulders and her arms, sliding up and down, kneading the stiff muscles, and soothed her enough that she closed her eyes.

She inhaled his deep, rich scent and pulled him closer. She'd missed this. Missed *him*.

He dropped a kiss on the top of her head. "I love you, Cora. Never stopped."

"I love you, too," she whispered, but she wasn't sure he heard her. She wasn't even sure she said it out loud.

They lay there for a long while, no words needed. Cora continued to wonder what Sam's last hours on earth were like. Had he even thought of his children? Wondered about how his life had turned out the way it did? Had he been with his fling of the week just hours before and not spared a single thought to the family he'd left behind?

Liam shifted. "I guess I need to get home. It's getting late."

Cora's insides screamed and her arms tightened around him. She'd deal with their relationship tomorrow.

"Please don't go."

He settled again. "I know you don't want me here over night, Cor."

"Maybe tonight I'll make an exception."

"I don't think that's a good idea. The kids just lost their dad."

Cora sat up and ran her hands down her face. Liam's soothing hand on her back didn't help the sorrow in her heart.

"You're right. They love you, but I have to be fair to them right now. I'm being selfish."

He smiled at her. "You're being human. I'll be back first thing in the morning."

When she started to object, he gently urged her chin toward him and looked her square in the eye. "You're not alone. You'll never be alone again."

"Promise?" She dared to hope again… maybe she'd regret it come morning, but right now, knowing she wasn't alone meant everything to her.

"Always."

The next morning, Liam woke up at his usual time. He sent Cora a brief text.

I'll see you soon.

As usual, she didn't respond. After his morning chores on the ranch, he pulled out of his driveway and headed for a drive through for breakfast. They might not want to eat, but it was important they all keep their strength up.

It wasn't until Liam pulled into her driveway he started growing anxious. Last night, Cora had been full of emotion. For a few moments, the walls had disintegrated, and it was just the two of them again.

Just like before.

Jolie met him at the door, her sad, hazel eyes void of

their usual sparkle.

"Why are you here?" she asked in a flat tone.

"I thought you guys could use some breakfast."

"Mom's not gonna be happy you just showed up again."

"I texted her earlier."

Uncharacteristically, Jolie rolled her eyes and stepped aside for him to enter. "You've been texting her for six months. Still doesn't mean anything."

Liam swallowed and then cleared his throat. How much had Cora told her? Jolie was always welcoming and kind to him. For now, he chalked it up to losing her father. That could make anyone lash out, even a kid as remarkable as her.

Walking to the kitchen, he rounded the corner just as Cora did and she bumped into him. Reaching out to steady her, he smiled a little.

"'Mornin, beautiful." He leaned forward and kissed her cheek, breathing deep.

Her mouth fell open into a little "o". "You shouldn't be here, Liam."

"I told you last night I was coming back this morning. And I sent you a text earlier."

Cora took the food and called the kids. The twins were the first to show up, and Jolie cautiously watched him as she unwrapped a biscuit.

"Jolie, could you please get your brothers something to drink? I'll just be a second."

Liam found himself being shoved out the front door onto the front portch by a woman half his size and twice his determination. She closed the door behind her.

"We need to talk."

"No," he drawled. "Cause I know that look, and talking is most definitely not what we need to do." He extended his arms and meant to pull her into a hug, but she took a step back.

"Last night was a mistake."

"And we're talking." Liam issued with a sarcastic tone and sighed. He placed his fingertips on his hips. "It doesn't have to be a mistake, Cora."

"But it was. My kids need me, and I can't do this with you right now."

"There's nothing to do. It's been a long six months without you. No more being apart. No more being scared. Either of us," he said pointedly.

She swallowed, looking panicked for a moment. But then she shook her head. "No. I meant it when I called...whatever this was, off. I can't be around you because it hurts too much."

"I love you." Maybe he was being simple thinking that was enough, but for him, it was. If she still loved him, he knew they could work out anything together.

"Sometimes love isn't enough." She looked out over the front yard as a car went by and closed herself off to him by crossing her arms under her breasts. "Some-times..." Cora's eyes met his. "Sometimes actions speak louder than words."

"Then let me prove it to you."

Cora's tongue darted out as she wet her lips. Then she turned and opened the front door, placing herself between the house and him.

"It's too late, Liam. We're over."

His anger surged, and his eyes narrowed. "I won't accept it."

"You have to. Go home. Thank you for breakfast, but I've got it from here."

She walked inside and the click of the door felt like a gunshot in the early morning air.

Sad. Final. Lifeless.

He'd suspected he'd be met with restraint if he tried to get close again.

He wouldn't let one setback stop him though.

Chapter Four

True love doesn't have a happy ending.
True love has no ending…

"WHAT DID HE want?" Jolie asked once Cora closed the front door.

"Just bringing breakfast for us. Being nice." Her tone was overly cheerful, and she knew her very alert daughter saw right through her. She disappeared into the kitchen, hoping that making some tea would calm her heart. She had no way of knowing if she'd made the right decision. She missed him but she couldn't live her life being pushed into something she wasn't ready for. Sam had taught her a long time ago the only person she could depend on was herself, and she had to love herself enough to protect her heart.

"Mom," Jolie said behind her, causing her to startle. "He hasn't been around in six months. Why is he showing up now?"

Cora spun to face her lovely, almost-grown daughter. Her dark hair was cropped to her shoulders and her large hazel eyes implored hers.

"Now isn't the time, sweetheart. We have a lot going on, especially you. How are you feeling this morning?"

"I'll be fine," she shrugged suddenly, averting her gaze. "I know you two broke up, but you never told me why. But judging from the fact he still texts you every morning and now he's coming back around, it tells me maybe you broke up with him. I thought you guys were really happy."

Clearing her throat, Cora then shrugged. "It's complicated. And how did you know he still texts me every morning?"

"Tell me, Mom."

She sighed and sat down at the breakfast table. Jolie followed suit. Cora took a few moments to gather the right words. "We had a big argument. He pushed me too hard. He wanted to start talking about marriage, but I balked and told him I didn't want to get married again right now. We both said some things we regret."

"You've always taught us forgiveness, Mom."

Cora's heart flip-flopped. "Yes. But I thought since we'd only been together for a year, he shouldn't be thinking so seriously. I guess I wanted him to be content with where we were."

Jolie nodded, her ancient eyes full of wisdom.

"You see, honey," Cora continued, "When I met your dad, I pushed him. I was in a bad situation at home, and I wanted to escape. I even bought my wedding dress before he proposed. I think he felt like he had to propose after that."

"I don't understand."

"When Liam and I first started dating, it was great. I never wondered how he felt. For once it wasn't me falling for a man and pushing them for something more. I was confident in his feelings."

"So what was the problem?"

"I know what happens when you push someone into something they're not ready for. The outcome is never good."

Jolie slowly nodded, picking at her cuticles. "Liam was a good guy, Mom. Do you ever think you should reconsider?"

"Every day."

"So if he wants to try again, what's stopping you?"

"It's been six months, honey. Yes, he still texts; yes, he came by. But I think I became a habit. An older woman paying attention to him when he was lonely and between blondes. We never really made sense."

"You guys were perfect for each other."

Cora let Jolie's words wash over her, remembering just for a moment how much they'd loved in only a year. Then she pushed those thoughts aside and stood.

"I don't mean to change the subject, but we really need to call the funeral home and set a time to make your dad's arrangements."

Jolie's eyes filled with tears. "I don't want to, Mom."

"I know, honey. He and I had our differences, but I wish we didn't have to do this either."

With a bowed head, Jolie went upstairs to get ready. The twins were quietly watching TV and finishing their breakfast.

And Cora took just a moment, while no one was watching, to allow her shoulders to fall in defeat.

LIAM KICKED THE wooden post next to him in frustration and stabbed his fingers through his hair. He turned around and kicked it again for good measure then slammed his truck door closed.

The woman was near impossible. Stubborn. Enough to make a grown man weep. If Liam didn't have his pride, he would have succumbed to exasperated snivels then and there. He'd made one mistake. One hiccup in their entire relationship, and he was paying a handsome price for it. To be older than him, Cora sure could be a petulant child sometimes.

But even then, he wished he could kiss the frown right off her face until she smiled. Cause when she smiled, she lit up the room. Her blue eyes sparkled. And sometimes she clapped her hands together in joy as she threw her head back and laughed.

Liam had fallen so deeply for her, he'd never really known what hit him. Now he was pretty sure she was a sorceress and had cast a spell on him. He either needed her back, or he needed to be free of her. Either way wasn't going to be easy. Not after his visit this morning. He couldn't stand the thought of hurting her, but that's exactly what he had done.

Regardless, in those rare moments, when her guard was down, he could see she still loved him just as much as he loved her. Their hearts called to each other in a way he'd never experienced. He'd laughed when a few of his friends talked about it in their own relationships. It seemed too cheesy to be real and just a figment of a lust-induced haze. In a new relationship, each party is always thinking of each other, right?

Liam was a believer. Cora was an extension of him. When she hurt, he hurt. When she needed him, he somehow knew. And while she was still really good at pretending she didn't want him, or anyone really, Liam called her bluff too many times to believe her anymore. It was the only thing keeping him going.

So tomorrow, he'd show up first thing in the morning and do it all over again. He'd prove to her she was the most important woman in the world to him. By the time she accepted the inevitable, and accept it she would, she wouldn't question him anymore. Cora would know, without a doubt, Liam was the man she was going to spend the rest of her life with.

Chapter Five

Life is a brief intermission between birth and death…enjoy it.

THE NEXT MORNING, Cora, weary-eyed and tired, woke to a knock on the door downstairs. Shrugging on her fuzzy robe and slippers, she said a quick prayer it was just the mailman dropping off a package. She'd kept the kids out of school again today so they could properly grieve their father on the eve of his burial. Strangely, the twins still seemed to show no signs of sadness, even when she'd let them pick out their father's casket yesterday. Cora knew everyone grieved differently, but she was starting to worry maybe they were holding too much in.

Rushing down the stairs, she heard the rumble of a low voice. Her worst fears were confirmed when she skidded to a halt and saw Liam standing just inside the door, breakfast in hand and a big smile on Jolie's face.

Her smile fell when she looked her mother's attire up and down.

"Cora," Liam said, the corners of his mouth twitching.

"Mom," Jolie hissed loud enough for everyone to hear and nodded upstairs. "Go brush your hair."

Looking around with a sinking feeling in her chest, she realized soon enough that Jolie was happy Liam was back in their life. The twins were sitting on the couch, taking turns from watching their morning cartoons to sending worshipped-filled gazes his way.

With a roll of her eyes, she padded back upstairs and got ready for the day. As if it wasn't hard enough to prepare the kids for their father's funeral, now she had to deal with Liam being everywhere.

After taking her time showering, Cora went back downstairs and saw Ashton, Aldin and Liam playing basketball outside. She frowned, wondering if it would seem disrespectful for them to be playing when their father was in a casket.

Jolie walked out of the kitchen. "They're having fun, Mom. Just because Dad is dead doesn't mean we have to be." Cora thought it was admirable how Jolie pushed passed the tremble in her voice to say what she needed to say.

Cora swallowed. "I love you, Jolie. You're so beautiful." Cora enveloped her in a big hug and squeezed as hard as she dared. "Inside and out. You're wise beyond your years. I'll never know why God wanted me to be your mama when you're the one teaching me about life and not the other way around."

"I'm sorry you're having to deal with everything. I wish I was eighteen and could take that off your plate. Having Liam here is hard enough without funerals and all the sadness."

Pulling back, Cora massaged Jolie's shoulders and made sure she looked her in the eye. "Liam is not what's important right now. You and your brothers are my world. You know that."

"I do. But I still hold on to hope that one day you and Liam can love each other again. I think he still loves you. I know he does. I can see it in his eyes. It's the way Scotty Dover looked at me all during freshman year."

Cora chuckled. "That boy had it bad for you."

"Liam has it bad for you."

"Maybe. But now isn't the time to be thinking about it."

"Mom?" Jolie hesitated and took a deep breath. "Will you promise me something?"

"Anything, honey."

"Will you let Liam be here for us? Whatever his reasons for coming over, can you just let him? When he's here, it feels like our family is complete again. And I know none of this is easy on you, either, but even the best mom in the world needs to let someone be there for her sometime."

Cora's arms fell to the side, and she pondered Jolie's words. There were times she felt like she was talking to her grandmother, not her sixteen-year-old daughter. To say she was an old soul was an understatement.

"I'll do my best."

Looking over Jolie's shoulder, Liam's penetrating green-eyed gaze caught hers through the window. He wore a backwards baseball hat, much like the time he'd cornered her in the grocery store just before she gave in and went out with him.

With a casual wink, one that suggested familiarity and knowing the direction of her thoughts, he slam-dunked the ball into the basket, laughing at the twins as they cheered and offered high fives.

For a moment, Cora let herself forget there was a chasm as big as the Atlantic between them. For a moment, she let herself remember the stunning moments, all the thoughtful words he'd spoken to her, words she'd taken to heart.

She wouldn't be stupid this time. Both eyes were open and none of his flowery words or perfectly timed texts would persuade her marriage was the answer.

She'd walked that road before. Never again.

Liam learned the wake for Sam would take place that night. Cora spent the afternoon going through closets to find tonight and tomorrow's funeral clothes. Around three, she came downstairs, hair askew and dark circles under her eyes.

She fell on the couch and sighed. "The boys have nothing to wear. We have to be at the funeral home in three hours, and they have nothing. Why didn't I think of this sooner?"

"Well, let's gather them up and head to the mall. We can grab an early dinner and go straight to the funeral home after."

Cora's eyes narrowed. "Why are you here? Nothing's changed."

"Maybe not, but that doesn't mean I don't still love you and the kids, and I'll do anything I can to make this easier on you."

She studied him for a moment, her face finally softening. "Fine. Let me go tell everyone." She stood and took a deep breath. Her blue eyes met his. A hesitant smile graced her lips.

Liam watched her work her way up the stairs, the soft sway of her hips making his mouth water.

Mercy, he loved that woman.

At the mall, Liam and Cora quickly found something suitable for the twins, paid for it and went straight to food court to get an early dinner. None of them were very hungry, but Liam bought their food and insisted everyone eat at least half of what was on their plate. Even Cora. She was Casper-pale. He worried she wasn't taking good care of herself. Come to think of it, he hadn't seen her eat or drink anything all day.

When he realized she was staring off into the distance, he placed his hand over hers and squeezed. "You need to eat, Cor."

She frowned and picked at her fries. Finally, she ate a small piece. Liam knew it couldn't be easy burying your first love, even if that love had been tainted with deception and cheating. And she was probably overwhelmed and didn't know how to help her kids. He was starting to worry about the twins. They had yet to show any grief over their father's passing.

They went back to Liam's house so he could change. It was closer to the funeral home anyway. The boys changed, and Cora helped them look their best. Cora wore a black dress, modest in length but still managed to look stunning. Jolie had purposefully chosen a flowered dress and had mentioned in the car that tomorrow she would wear black. Tonight was about celebrating her father.

Sometimes, Liam was in awe over that kid. Cora was one amazing mother to raise her the way she did.

When he realized Cora was missing, he turned the living room TV on for the kids and told them he'd be right back.

He found her in his master bathroom, sitting on the side of the tub, head in hands.

"Hey," he said quietly so as not to startle her. "You okay?" It was a dumb question, but he hoped she'd open up to him.

"No. Married or not, I never really thought about burying him. I kind of assumed he'd be around forever."

"Time has a way of showing us who's boss, huh?"

She grunted in response.

"Do you need anything?"

Cora sat up and squared her shoulders. Then she stood in front of him. "I need a hug." She walked straight into his arms, not even considering the fact he would deny her. She pressed her ear against his chest and wrapped her arms around his waist. He smoothed her hair and kissed her forehead.

"I can hear your heart beating," she whispered.

He knew she was struggling with her own mortality, her own grief. So he said nothing. Now wasn't the time for flowery words or promises of forever despite the overwhelming need to say it. He wanted to just be there for her and help her through this, even if it was just as friends.

Without warning, Cora lifted her arms and pulled his head down as she stood on her tiptoes and touched her lips to his. It wasn't a kiss meant to entice or provoke, but rather he could sense her desperation. The need to feel. To know they were both alive.

She didn't take it any further than just their mouths pressed together and soon enough, she tore away from him and walked out of the room. He'd barely had time to register what was happening before she was already gone.

He took his time making his way back to the living room, gathering his wits and making a game plan. He hadn't even asked Cora if it was okay for him to come to the wake, but then again, she hadn't refused him either when he'd made his intentions clear. Rather, she'd seem to calmly accept his presence and for that, he was grateful.

She stood guard over the kids, arms crossed and face closed, pretending to watch TV, but he knew she wasn't really seeing anything. Wrestling with humanity didn't allow for such luxuries. He'd been there before, back when his dad died a few years back. He'd never felt so exposed, so alone than when the one person he'd always taken for granted was just a memory.

And now, in more ways than one, all of Cora's past was now a memorial. A commemoration treasured only for the good times with the bad times soon forgotten.

Liam walked up behind her and rubbed the stiffness from her shoulders, trying to bring her back to reality.

"We should go, Cor."

Throwing a hesitant smile over her shoulder, she took a deep breath. Then she turned to the three pair of eyes watching her expectantly. "Time to leave, kids."

Slowly, the twins stood and walked to the door first. Jolie took a little longer, as if reluctant to finally say goodbye to her father again. Her young features were pinched, closed off just like her mother's. She took smaller steps, dragging out the length of time it took to walk from the couch to the front door.

Cora hung back, just like a shepherd tending a flock. She, too, took slower steps to the door, but her arms uncrossed and she squared her shoulders. That was her, his Cora. Always pushing herself to go a little further, step out of her comfort zone and put aside her own fears to take care of those she loved.

Liam loved that about her. Sometimes he wished he was as strong as her. He'd watched her on more than one occasion take the lead even when she was lost and fighting to find her own way.

With his hand on the small of her back, he allowed them all to take their time making their way to his truck. Cora's gaze stayed on the ground, yet he yearned to help her look up again. Feel the sun on her skin.

In her own time, Cora would rise like a phoenix from the ashes and begin to live her life again.

Liam just prayed there was a place for him in it.

Chapter Six

Running from your problems is a race you'll never win…

THE FUNERAL HOME reeked of too-sweet carnations and formaldehyde. The wallpaper was a cheery scroll pattern that belied the somberness of the occasion. The director took them into his office and gave them a mechanical smile. Cora couldn't help but glare at him. It wasn't *his* life falling apart.

"Again, I'd like to extend my deepest sympathies to you and your family. I know it's hard to lose your husband."

"Ex…husband," she murmured. She failed to mention this was her second time to say goodbye to him.

The director shook her hand and then Jolie's and moved to the twins. He turned to Liam, extending his hand and said, "And you are?"

Liam cast a quick look her way and pressed his lips together. "Moral support."

"Very well. When you guys are ready, I'll take you back to see him. There's no rush. You just come outside when you're ready."

Cora turned to her kids, ignoring the savage nausea wrestling in her throat. She swallowed it down and gave her kids a smile to let them know she was still here. Not everyone had disappeared.

Jolie's eyes were bright. "Mom…"

"I know, sweetheart. Take your time."

"I don't know if I can see him like that."

Cora pulled Jolie into her arms. "You can, and you will. You might not want to do this now, but one day you'll be glad you got to say goodbye."

The twins, once again stood waiting, quiet, strangely unemotional. Cora made a mental note to talk to them after the wake to see how they were doing. Jolie tended to express her feelings easier. But the twins held everything in more or talked to each other.

Like a rock, Liam stood by the door, waiting on them, patient as ever. Her defenses were down, but she wanted nothing more than for his strong, steely arms to wrap her in a tight hug and not let go until morning. She needed his strength now more than ever.

The director walked them down the short hall in front of the double doors. Behind those doors lay the body of a man she'd fallen in love with, married, shared fifteen years of her life with, created three remarkable lives…It hardly seemed fair his world had came to a screeching halt at the hands of a drunk driver. The details surrounding the accident were still being uncovered, but only one important thing was in front of them.

Sam was dead.

At her nod, the director opened the door. She looked into the pink-lit room and saw Sam's familiar profile above the edge of the opened casket. His eyes were closed in rest. He'd always had the straightest nose of anyone she'd ever seen, full lips she now knew would never smile or say I love you to their children again.

Cora waited to feel something. A rush of sadness. A choke of tears. An overwhelming sense of loss. But she stood there, as dead on the inside as her ex-husband lying in his casket.

Then, Liam's warm fingers slipped into hers and squeezed. Her heart thawed enough for a small hiccup of emotion to work its way into her throat in the form of a lump she had to swallow past.

Sam would miss seeing the kids' first dates. Their high school and college graduation. Soccer games, basketball games. First dates. Everything that, years ago, they'd once dreamed about sharing together, excited for their future.

On the other side, Jolie's hand slipped into hers and squeezed, just as Liam's had. The twins stood hand in hand and Ashton held out his hand to Jolie. As a family, because in that moment, that's what they were, they took the first steps to say good-bye to the man they all loved in some way. Together, one step at a time, they drew closer to Sam. Jolie's grasp on her hand tightened. A quick glance and Cora watched her lower her head, a tear finally slipping down her precious cheek.

At the casket, Cora took the first look. Her ex-husband, the man who'd become a stranger to her over the years, looking nothing like the many mornings she'd rolled over and watched him sleep, completely in love with their life together. His face was peaceful, only marred by a single cut on his temple from the accident. If nothing else, she prayed he'd found his eternal rest. He even had the slight curl to his lips, like he held a secret no one else knew. For a moment, Cora smiled.

In some ways, death could be beautiful. Tragic. Full of hope that what was to come in the after life was as magnificent as the moments they'd shared together on Earth.

Sam, for all his faults, had been a good man; a good man who had made a lot of bad decisions and didn't know how to crawl out of the hole from which he'd mined. His decisions had had consequences, that to some extent, they were all still suffering. It seemed unfair in his peaceful slumber they should all be left to pick up his broken pieces.

But in the end, he'd tried to change his life. He'd been giving Jolie more time, taking the twins to hit balls at the park. He'd been trying. And that was all Cora had ever wanted.

The lump in her throat formed again. She viciously swallowed. Raising her eyes from her ex-husband's face, her eyes filled with tears, but they didn't fall. She stared into the blurring background of Sam's casket and willed them gone. Liam's thumb traced reassuring circles on the back of her hand. If she turned to him for a hug she desperately needed, the tears would drop and she had to be stronger than that for her kids.

Untangling Liam's fingers from hers, immediately feeling the loss of his support, Cora put her arms around Jolie as she stepped forward a little. Silent tears flowed down Jolie's face, her carefully applied makeup streaked with mascara smudges and completely removed in other areas where she'd tried to scrub her face clean. In an instant, a tissue was under her nose. Looking up, Jolie smiled her thanks at Liam and took the tissue he offered. She dabbed at her tears and looked back down to her father.

"He looks peaceful," Cora offered, wishing Jolie would say something.

"When I woke up this morning I prayed this would all be a bad dream."

Cora cleared her throat to dislodge the tears threatening for her oldest child.

"But seeing him lying here, I just...I can't." Jolie reached out and laid her hands on top her fathers. Cora noticed then how they had the same hands. Clean squared nails with long fingers.

Jolie's sweet face crumpled and she turned to Cora, sobbing quietly. Behind her, Cora could see the twins standing at a distance, their eyes anywhere but on their father. Giving Liam a meaningful look, he moved to take Jolie into his arms while Cora went over to the boys.

Ashton and Aldin looked at her curiously but didn't say anything. "We don't want to see him, Mom," Aldin said. His voice was strong and sure.

"Honey, you need to say goodbye. It's hard, I know, but right now is your only chance to say anything you want to say to him."

"He left us. He hurt you. He hurt Jolie," Ashton continued. "I say good riddance."

"Ashton!" Appalled, Cora stood speechless looking into her son's suddenly icy eyes.

Aldin gave his brother a look and they nodded. "We don't want to see him, Mom. We've made up our mind."

Rarely did Cora come up empty on how to handle her kids. She wasn't perfect, but usually she could get through a situation. This time, she had nothing.

"Boys," Liam said stepping in, "It's okay if you don't want to see him right now. You have until tomorrow to change your mind, but I agree with your mother. Even if you don't want to see him, one day you might be pretty sad you didn't get to. After tomorrow, you'll only see him in your mind and in pictures. Never again in person."

Cora was relieved when the boys said nothing but rather turned and went back into the lobby, sitting down next to each other.

"Thank you," Cora mumbled to Liam, overwhelmed.

"Anytime. I'll keep an eye on them tonight while you're with Jolie. The boys are angry. I get that. I was pretty angry with my dad for leaving me, too."

Cora's jaw dropped. All this time she'd been wrapped up in their own situation, and she'd forgotten Liam had lost his father a few years ago.

"Oh, Liam, I'm so sorry. I wasn't even thinking. I know this has to be hard for you and bringing back–"

His fingers whispered against her cheek and he brushed a kiss into her hair. His arms wrapped around her shoulders and pulled her in fiercely but briefly. "I'm fine. None of this is about me, baby."

"Still, I'm sorry you had to come. But I'm glad you're here."

Tenderly, Liam's index finger hooked under her chin and forced her gaze to his. "You're my favorite place to be."

LIAM'S SPIDEY SENSES were tingling with the twins. He remembered all too well how easy it was to become angry over life's curveballs. When his father had passed, he'd had ample time to prepare. He'd had cancer for two years, giving him plenty of time to say anything that needed to be said. But Liam distinctly remembered taking a hammer to the old tree house they'd built when he was a kid and destroying it until nothing was left but splintered wood. Then he'd cried every time he passed it for six months because it had been one of the few things left they'd done together that held some memories of the two of them. After that, he'd become a typical know-it-all teenager too good to spend time with his own father.

Hindsight was always 20/20.

Liam straddled the room and the hallway where Cora and Jolie greeted guests where he could also keep a close eye on the twins in the lobby. A few other kids arrived, and they went outside to play for a while. Liam watched Cora graciously receive guests for her ex-husband. He wasn't sure if he was in her shoes if he could do it. He'd never liked Sam, not even a little. And seeing how Cora was handling things, he disliked him even more because the man had put her through hell. And now she was ushering him into the afterlife like he was a saint.

The man had cheated on her. Slept with other women while they were married. Emotionally abused her. Neglected his kids. Liam supposed those things were easily forgotten when she was drowning in the thick of his wake. It seemed the twins hadn't forgotten though.

Regardless, Cora was right. Sam was their father, and they needed to say goodbye. Maybe after everyone left, the director would give them a few more minutes with Sam's body so they could do what needed to be done.

Liam was proud of Jolie. She stood next to the coffin with Cora, smiling and greeting guests with her usual smile. Seeing her father's body maybe hadn't gotten easier, but she had adapted, strong and sure, just like her mother and stood with grace and composure even a real-life princess could admire.

At one point, Cora searched the room until she found him. When their eyes met, he could have sworn he saw them light up just a bit and a hint of a welcoming smile played on her mouth.

Liam wasn't fool enough to think all was forgotten between them. Right now, she was high on emotion, and Liam would do well to remember that.

He walked over to the water cooler and poured Cora and Jolie a cup of water. Then he walked up to Cora and kissed her temple. "You two need anything else? Tissues?"

Cora's hands surrounded the glass as she took a long drink. Her fingers came up and played with his collar, straightening his tie. "We're good." For a brief moment, her eyes crashed into his, and she smiled a sad, lonely smile. "I appreciate this."

Now and probably not anytime soon wasn't the time for them to talk about their relationship. Per usual, Sam had thrown a monkey wrench in his carefully laid plans of winning back the love of his life. Liam supposed he couldn't rightfully be mad right now with the man lying in a casket. He couldn't do much else from the grave.

Liam could be patient. He would be patient. He had to be patient.

"Daddy!" a boy behind him called. He ran into the receiving room at a break neck pace. It was one of the boys the twins were outside playing with.

The man shushed him, but the little boy was frantic.

"Ashton and Aldin disappeared! We were playing hide and seek near the woods, and we looked and looked for them but we couldn't find them anywhere. We called their name and everything."

Liam heard Cora's sharp intake of breath.

Liam held up his hands. "I told them they could play outside. I'll take care of it. I'm sure they're just hiding really well. Don't worry." He bent to make eye contact with Cora to reiterate what he was saying. The last thing she needed was more anxiety. She'd break.

Rushing outside, Liam ran to the edge of the parking lot and called for the twins. Five minutes later, he was still walking through the woods calling their names. Before long, the setting sun made the woods much darker than he would like with two eleven year olds missing. He could hear a few others behind him calling their names.

When he came up empty over a mile into the trees, Liam rushed back to the funeral home when he heard the distant sound of sirens. Maybe one of them had been hurt. He ran as fast as he could, imagining the worst for the boys who had stolen his heart two years ago.

In the parking lot, Cora stood, worrying her hands, her hair askew. Jolie was crying again and the police were talking to Cora. A sinking feeling in Liam's gut caused him to stop running and come to a stand still.

When Cora's saw him, she rushed straight into his arms and burst into tears.

"They're gone, Liam! The twins are missing!"

Chapter Seven

*Never fear shadows. They simply mean there's
a light shining somewhere...*

LIAM TRIED NOT to let his panic show. Cora was too pale. Jolie was sobbing. The twins were somewhere out there, hurting, maybe not just emotionally. The cops, oddly enough the same two who had broken the news of Sam's death in Cora's living room, questioned him and Cora about the twins disappearance. The little boy they'd been playing with also told them all he remembered.

The twins left no sign or hint of where they might have gone. Liam took a second to walk away from the crowd that had gathered and tried to think. Years ago, he'd been in this very position, albeit a little older. So where would two young boys, who only had each other, go to in order to be alone?

Liam paced. They wouldn't go back home. Too obvious and they were probably afraid of getting in trouble by now. Stabbing his fingers through his hair, he gritted his teeth. *Think.*

He tried to put himself in their shoes, but he'd missed so much in the last six months he wasn't sure he knew them as well as he once had. One thing he knew for certain: Ashton and Aldin had solid heads on their shoulders. They would be okay, of that he had no doubt.

Rejoining Cora's side, he took her hand in his as a silent show of support. He wasn't sure if she even realized he was there as distraught as she was, but he loved those boys and was determined to bring them home safe. He wouldn't admit it, but he was just as rattled as her. Those boys, Cora and Jolie were his life.

"Cora, I think you should go home and wait for them in case they come back home. I'm gonna go out with the cops and look for them."

She stiffened next to him. "I'm not going anywhere. They might have gotten lost and they're trying to find their way."

Liam took her shoulders in his hands and lowered himself to her level. "You need to wait for them. In case they call, in case they come home." In case you collapse, he didn't add. She was shivering head to toe and her lips were pale. The dark circles under her eyes told him she hadn't been sleeping well.

Her eyes filled with tears. "Please don't make me. I'm closer to them here."

Giving her a fierce hug, he then took her face in his hands and forced her gaze up to his. "The next time I see you, the twins will be safely home. I'm not coming back until we have them, Cora. I promise."

Doubt warred with hope in the depths of her blue eyes. She was looking to him to make everything okay. He might have made some mistakes, but he couldn't afford to fail this time. The twins needed him. Cora needed him.

Liam placed a tender kiss on Cora's lips. Touching his forehead to hers, he whispered, "I love you. I love those boys. Everything is going to be fine."

"Bring them home, Liam. I need my boys home."

"Wait for me there."

With a final hug, Liam ushered Cora and Jolie to her car and gave the keys to a friend standing near by, asking for them to take her home. No way was he allowing either of them to drive home right now. Cora started to protest, but he stood his ground and finally won.

When the tail lights faded into the distance and he was sure they were going to get home safe, Liam turned to the police and the rescue team being formed, helping them formulate a plan based on what he knew about the boys.

With a deep breath, he sent up a silent prayer. *Please let them be safe.*

Hour after hour passed. Darkness settled so thick around them Liam could taste it. No sign. No word. Not a sound. At least a hundred people were searching for two little boys.

Every tree he rounded came up empty. He tripped over tree roots and thought about how easy it would be for the boys to both get hurt when the moon wasn't out. Sweat trickled down his back and into his eyes, stinging.

Liam was beginning to fear the worst. Maybe someone had snatched them. But he refused to go there until the police said they should. He had to believe after their angry state at the wake they were probably trying to run from their grief.

Grief born from unexpected pain was the worst kind. At least he'd had time to prepare for his father's passing. At least he'd still had the tree house he'd built as a reminder, even if it was in splinters. Each nail on the ground was one his father had touched. Something that connected him to his father even after his passing…

Then, like the force of a thousand suns, a thought rose to the surface. He'd wanted to feel connected to his father. The last thing they'd done together…

Hadn't Cora mentioned Sam taking them on a lakeside lunch last weekend?

On a hunch, Sam turned and ran to his car. The lake was about three miles from the funeral home. Within walking distance for the twins if they really wanted to go. He burned rubber pealing out of the parking lot and exceeded the speed limit three times over to get to his boys.

There was a huge hill at the lake. One or both of the twins could have fallen. He suddenly realized he had no idea if the twins knew how to swim. What if they fell into the lake?

Liam's breath came in short huffs as he pulled into the state park. He threw the truck into park and jumped out, not bothering to close the driver's side door.

They'd searched all night and the sunrise created brilliant pink and purple hues in the sky as the rays of first light stretched and welcomed the morning. Skidding and slipping down the hill, Liam went as fast as he could. When he finally reached the bottom he looked to the left and saw the playground.

Empty.

His heart pounded harder.

He looked to his right. Against the morning sky, stood two perfect little boy silhouettes on the lakeshore, skipping rocks. He blinked to make sure he wasn't imagining things. He'd gone all night without sleep and his eyes burned.

When they didn't disappear, Liam took a second to compose himself. He had to remember they were grieving. Maybe more than Jolie or Cora. There was something special about the bond between a boy and his father, just like with a girl and her mother. An innate understanding of one another.

Slowly, Liam made his way to the boys. They were talking quietly as he approached.

"Boys?" he called.

Ashton and Aldin turned to him. Then, as if deciding to ignore his presence, they turned and gathered more stones.

Finally, he was close enough to see them in the lightening sky. "You gave your mother and sister and me a big scare."

Still they said nothing. Ashton attempted to skip a rock but it plunked in the water.

"Dad taught us how to skip rocks last weekend. But now neither of us can do it."

The raw emotion in Aldin's voice bordered on hysteria.

Ashton turned to him after another rock plunked down, his face empty.

"I could show you," Liam offered.

"No. This was Dad's thing. He taught us. Not you." Ashton's stance told Liam he was ready to fight.

Liam held his hands up in surrender. "I get it."

"No, you don't. You made Mom cry, too. *You're* no better than him."

Taking a deep breath, Liam dug deep to gather his patience and swallowed down a protest. Defending himself right now wasn't what either of them needed.

"Your mom is really worried. I told her I'd find you and bring you home."

Aldin spoke up, "How did you find us?"

"Well, I lost my dad once, too. And something your mom said reminded me of something I did. So I thought I'd give it a shot. I'm glad I did. I'd never be able to forgive myself if something happened to you boys."

"Why did you leave us?" Aldin asked, tears thick in his voice.

"It's complicated, son."

"We aren't your sons. Never will be." Ashton threw one last rock at the lake and headed for the big hill where his truck was, stomping past Liam. Aldin followed, but cast him a furtive glance, making sure he was following them.

Once they were all in the car and buckled, Liam grabbed the steering wheel until his knuckles turned white. "I'm sorry I left you boys. I never wanted to. Your mom and I had some things we needed to work out and then things got messy. But I can promise you, with all my heart, I'm not going anywhere this time."

Perhaps it was too soon to make such a promise aloud to them, but Liam vowed to himself then and there, no matter where his relationship with Cora wound up, he'd always be there for her kids.

"I lost my dad a few years ago, too. I was angry, just like you. But, man to man, if you only hear one thing that I say, please hear this. You have to say goodbye to your father. You're not getting rid of his memory or him. But it's the last time you'll see him. It'll help you heal. It'll make things easier. It won't erase the pain; that comes with time. But having peace is the last gift your father can give you."

The rest of the ride was spent in silence. It was after 6:00 a.m. when he pulled in Cora's driveway. His eyes felt like sandpaper and the boys had both fallen asleep. He nudged them and they all exited the car.

The twins trudged toward the house like they were walking to the death chamber. Liam bit back a chuckle. He remembered the days well when he feared his mother's punishment.

Ashton pushed the front door open and Aldin followed him in. Liam finished up the text he was sending to the head of the rescue team and walked in just as Cora and Jolie sat up on the couch, bleary eyed and confused. Clearly Jolie was the only one who'd slept.

Then, reality returned, and Cora's eyes lit up. She jumped from the couch and ran to the twins and took them both into her arms. She cried gut-wrenching sobs that broke his heart. Cries only a mother could weep for her children. Tears of relief after the darkest storm.

She showered them with kisses. "Where did you go? Why did you leave?"

Ashton looked to Liam. After his talk with them in the car, something seemed to have shifted. He hadn't won their trust again, but they had a mutual agreement for now.

Liam nodded to Ashton.

"Dad taught us to skip rocks last weekend. We wanted to go to the lake."

Cora was still sluggish enough all the dots hadn't connected just yet. He'd explain later. "Why don't you boys go get some sleep? We can talk about this some more after we've all had some rest."

Jolie gave each of her brothers a long hug after Cora released them and followed them upstairs.

Cora slowly rose from the floor and faced him. Her face crumpled again and she rushed into his arms, knocking him a few steps back. "Thank you," she blubbered into his shirt. "I don't know how you found them, but thank you."

Liam pulled her hair from her face and smoothed it back, holding on to her tight. They stood there for a long time, her tears finally quieting to hiccups.

It was Liam who pulled away first and took her face in his hands. "I told you everything was going to be fine."

Cora's hand came up and hooked around his wrists. Her blue eyes bounced back and forth between his, like she was peering into his soul. "Thank you for bringing them home."

Gently, he pressed his lips to hers, then pulled away.

"You must be exhausted," she finally said. "Go lie down. I don't want you to drive this tired."

Liam grinned. He loved it when she protected him.

"How about we both lie down. I can't imagine you slept well."

She gave him a hesitant glance.

He held his hands up in surrender. "Purely for sleep purposes. I couldn't do anything else if I wanted to."

Cora's shoulders slumped, and she smiled, clearly relieved. "Okay."

She followed him into her bedroom, and he collapsed on top of the mattress, not bothering to remove his shoes. He closed his eyes and felt the edges of sleep just as a gentle tug on his boots stirred him.

Cora was removing his shoes. It was an act of service, one that yanked at his heart. She was just as tired as he was, maybe more, but yet she still loved him enough to think of him before herself. It was in that moment Liam realized he let her doubt his feelings again. He'd never met a woman as selfless and amazing as the woman before him.

"Come here," he murmured and held out his arms. She crawled to the other side of him then settled in his arms. Liam took a deep breath and sent up a prayer of thanks, for finding the twins, for their sister, for the woman he now held...

For every step of his life that lead him straight to them.

Chapter Eight

The light at the end of the tunnel is your life;
it's the tunnel that's temporary…

CORA WOKE TO the uncanny feeling she was being watched. Cracking an eye open, she looked straight into her favorite pair of green eyes. Liam. He was still there. The boys were home safe because of him.

"Good…" he glanced at his watch, "evening," he said with a smile. He lay next to her, propping his head on his temple as he looked down on her.

"How are you even awake? I feel like I've been hit by a bus."

Liam chuckled. "Ranch life trained me well."

Cora closed her eyes again, intent on going back to sleep. Jolie was no doubt keeping a close eye on the boys if they weren't still asleep themselves.

When Liam's fingertips trailed against her jawline, she looked up at him to see his features softened and love shining in his eyes.

"I'm sorry, Cora."

He was talking about more than just the past twenty-four hours, but she played dumb. She couldn't have a deep conversation with him right now. She needed to see her boys and make everyone dinner. Tomorrow morning was Sam's funeral and she needed to have a sit down discussion with her children to make sure they understood she was there for them.

"Don't be silly. All's well that ends well, right?" She sat up, ready to flee, but he grabbed her wrist, pulling her back down. He was immediately over her, his arm around her waist. She was pinned down, and he wouldn't let her go anywhere until he was ready.

"I never meant to hurt you. I shouldn't have pushed you about marriage."

Such a simple statement for such a complex situation.

"I know. It's fine. I need to go see the boys."

Liam's evergreen gaze dropped to her mouth as he hovered above her. "It's not fine, Cor. I know life has never been easy on you, but I need you to know I never wanted you to do something you weren't ready for. "

"We all love each other in different ways, Liam. If nothing else, we make great friends." She pushed a little at his shoulders, feeling the panic in her throat threaten her air supply.

He shook his head. "We're not just friends, and you know it. It'll never be enough for either of us."

"Liam, let me go."

"We need to talk about this."

"I don't want to talk." Cora knew she was pouting like a five year old, but Liam brought it out of her. He knew exactly what he was doing to her, and he did it on purpose.

A delicious smile lifted the corners of his mouth and his eyes crinkled with mischief. "Don't want to talk, huh?"

"That's not what I—"

Before Cora fully registered what was happening, Liam's body was settling against hers, and his lips were descending, effectively halting her protest. She thought for a brief second about turning her head, but like Satan's lure to the fruit, Liam was irresistible.

Just before their mouths united, he pulled back to look her in the eyes. "I love you."

He didn't give her a chance to respond. His kiss was slow and deep, her lungs finally finding air on a sharp inhale. She'd known it for over two years now, but their attraction to each other was volatile. Like explosives lighting up a peaceful night. Cora didn't think she would ever understand it. How could two people so wrong for each other be so utterly right?

She couldn't give in to him. It wasn't the right time. She had to help her children grieve and maybe after that they could talk.

With a growl, Liam turned his head. Then he looked down at her and sighed. "For a few seconds there, you were right with me. Then you let reality set in again, didn't you?"

He knew her so well. Too well. No use in denying it. When she nodded, his mouth twisted into a wry smile. "It's frustrating as all get out, but it's part of why I love you. I get it." He rolled himself off her. "Go see how the twins are doing."

Cora sat up, suddenly unsure. Was she being fair to Liam? Did they have a future? Should she be kissing him when she wasn't sure if she could trust him with her heart again?

She angled a glance over her shoulder. "I'm sorry. Maybe you should go home."

"Nothing to be sorry for. And I'm not going any-where. Not until the funeral is over and I know you're okay. Maybe not even then."

When her surprised eyes clashed with his, he winked and crossed his ankles, throwing his arms behind his head. He was toying with her, but she couldn't help but grin back.

And her heart couldn't help but race.

LIAM HATED TIES. He hated suits. He hated dress shoes. He'd rather be in his T-shirt, jeans, and boots back at the ranch, knee deep in horse crap. He'd rather be *anywhere* than a funeral, especially this one.

Seeing Jolie so torn up over her father's death as she looked at him one last time caused a lump the size of Texas to lodge in his throat and hang on for dear life. The twins were still hanging back and he kept his eye on them in case they decided to dash again. This was their time before the funeral, just the family, to say their goodbyes. Liam couldn't help but feel like he was intruding on their private moment.

He observed Cora carefully for any signs of distress, but since the twins had been found, she'd seemed more herself. Her eyes were dry as she held Jolie up, whispering words only she could hear. Knowing Cora, she was reminding Jolie of all the good times and trying to help her eldest child forget the few years their father hadn't been himself. That was just the way she was. Forgiving, loving…always thinking the best of everyone.

Movement in the corner of the room caught his eye and he saw the twins put their arms around each other's shoulder, eyes downcast. His feet moved him toward them before he even thought about it.

They weren't babies anymore. At eleven, they understood everything. Being in the awkward pre-teen years didn't help the situation, especially since Cora had been mother and father for the last year. Sam had started stepping up, but a visit on the weekends wasn't enough for two twin boys learning how to be a man.

Liam ushered them to a seat. "Remember what we talked about yesterday in the car?"

"Yeah," Aldin said, scratching his nose.

Ashton studied his face. "Did you say goodbye to your dad when he died?"

"I did," Liam confirmed. "I won't lie. It wasn't easy seeing him lying there. I tried to remember that was just his body. Not really him. His essence, the part that made him *him*, went on to a better place."

Aldin's eyes were bright with unshed tears. Ashton nudged him, giving him a withering look.

"You know," Liam began again, "if there's one place you can cry without judgment, it's a funeral. It's better to get it out than hold it in."

Ashton snickered. "Like you ever cry."

"I do. I have. I sobbed like a baby when my dad died and everyone saw it." Liam looked around. "But nobody's here except us. Now's your chance." With a wink and a little grin, Liam stood. They might not want to say good-bye, but they had to.

Aldin looked up at him. "I know I'm eleven...but would you hold my hand? And don't leave me?"

The lump in Liam's throat was back with a vengeance. "Of course." His small hand slipped into his, and they walked together to Sam. As they were nearing, he felt a second hand on his other side creep into his. He gave them both a reassuring squeeze and smile.

When their approach caused Cora to turn, her eyes rounded and filled with tears. Jolie stepped away for her brothers to say their goodbyes and Cora joined them.

For a moment, the twins stood there, eyes glued to Sam's sleeping face. Aldin's tears fell silently down his face but Ashton was still stone cold.

"Say anything you've ever wanted to say. Good or bad," Liam urged. "You'll regret it if you don't."

Aldin pulled his hand from Liam's and took a step forward. He looked up at Cora, and she gave him an encouraging smile.

Aldin's gangly body inhaled deeply. "Hi, Dad. Thank you for teaching us how to skip rocks last weekend at the lake. I had fun spending time with you." His voice cracked.

He swallowed thickly then continued, "I'm gonna miss you, Dad. I was looking forward to all the things we talked about doing this summer. Paddle boats, fishing, camping…I guess that won't happen now, will it? But I'll be good for Mama, and I'll make good grades on all my schoolwork and be nice to Ashton and Jolie. If you can hear me, I want you to know I loved you. Even during the bad times. I forgive you for being mean to Mama. We're all gonna be okay." His hand reached inside his coat pocket and pulled out a small object. "I'll never forget you, Dad."

Aldin placed the object in Sam's coat pocket. As he placed it there, Liam saw it was a smooth stone. It was probably something he'd taken from the lakeshore. After the rock was with his father, Aldin turned to Cora and buried his face in her stomach, crying quietly.

Liam wasn't a crier, but such a sweet goodbye from such a sweet boy had been all he needed for tears to trail down his cheeks. So much of Cora was in him it stunned him. He was a forgiving boy, loving and kind. He would heal with Cora's love. If he admitted it to himself, he hoped he would be given a chance to love those boys until the day he was in a casket himself.

Ashton stepped up. His brown hair was askew and his tie was crooked, but he put his hands in his pockets and walked up to where Aldin had stood only moments before.

He took longer to start speaking. He scrutinized Sam with cold eyes, from head to toe, but after a while Liam could see his demeanor change. His shoulders slumped.

"You were a crappy dad. I hate you."

Cora took a step forward but Liam grabbed her hand and pulled her against him. "Let him be," he whispered against her temple. It was no doubt hard for Cora to see her son hurting, but he knew from experience, this needed to happen.

Ashton took a second for those words to sink in, like he was waiting for his father to wake up and respond.

When he didn't, he kept going, "I hate you. I hate how you treated Jolie. I hate how you made Mom do everything for you and you never said thank you. How Aldin was your favorite. How you missed my basketball games because you had a new girlfriend. I hate how you only had time for us on Saturdays and never any other day."

His hands came out of his pocket, and he studied his nails. Then he looked back into his father's face and tears filled his eyes. "I hate you, Daddy. I hate you left us. I hate you won't be here to see me win the next level of my video game. I hate how we never had enough time together before we had to say goodbye again." His words were broken between his cries, but he didn't stop.

"I wanted you to be a good dad. I wanted you to smile and be happy to see me. Why couldn't you be happy to see me? You always acted like I was just a chore, something you had to do. Well guess what? I had feelings, and you hurt them. I used to sit in my room and cry at night because I didn't think you loved me. I used to be scared for you to die because I was afraid it would be before I could show you I was good enough."

His face grew solemn. "I'm not scared anymore, Dad." With a great heave, Ashton punched the side of the coffin. His legs bent, and he doubled over as the loudest, most pitiful wails Liam had ever heard came from somewhere deep inside Ashton. Liam rushed to Ashton's side and pulled the boy into his arms, trying to let him know he wasn't alone.

"I hate you," Ashton gasped. "I just wanted a real dad!"

Liam cupped his hand over his head and held him close. Together they cried until Ashton was spent, his face blotchy and damp. When he finally pulled away from Liam, he looked back to Sam.

His voice still trembled as he whispered with finality, "Goodbye, Dad."

Chapter Nine

Every storm runs out of rain, and
every dark night turns into day...

SOMETHING BETWEEN THEM had shifted over the last few weeks. Cora sensed it, but like a true gentleman, Liam didn't mention it. Instead, he was there for them, never leaving even when she knew he had responsibilities at his ranch. He took care of the boys, gave them the laughter and time they deserved.

She'd learned that even in times of devastating sorrow, there were still precious moments of laughter to be had. Because they still had each other. They were still a family. Liam was a part of them.

Just like he'd said earlier, being friends wasn't enough. Slowly, ever so slowly, she had opened her heart to him and she found herself falling in love all over again, not that she'd ever stopped.

The twins came bursting into the house in their usual loud way and high fived each other then Liam. They smelled like a month old pair of dirty gym socks, and she ushered them upstairs for a shower with a grin.

Turning, Liam stood in the doorway watching her, a

look of pure contentment on his face.

"How can I ever thank you for all you've done for me and my kids?" She wandered over to him and took his hands in hers. He seemed surprised at her touch at first, looking down at their entwined fingers that fit perfectly together. Then he angled a sad look at her.

She knew what he was thinking somehow. They still hadn't talked about their fight or her reasons for not wanting to get married again.

Funny, after the events of the last few weeks, she was having trouble remembering any of them. Looking at Liam, the man who'd loved her and her kids through it all, she saw only her future. And she knew now that marriage between them was inevitable.

Love was a lot like fishing…she'd waited and waited for the line to catch, but now she had to decide if it was big enough to keep.

And Liam was a keeper.

"What?" he asked, his brows furrowing.

She grinned. Then it blossomed into a full-fledged smile, and her heart felt like it might burst. "I seem to recall you have a question to ask me."

His sparkling green eyes bounced back and forth between hers, clearly confused. The moment it dawned on him, his jaw dropped open a little.

"Are you sure?"

She nodded.

"Marry me."

Cora cocked a playful eyebrow. "That's wasn't a question."

"'Cause if I don't demand it, I'm afraid you'll figure a way out."

"Not gonna happen. Not this time. "

Cora thought of all they'd been through together and couldn't help but smile. He was still here. She might have gotten spooked, but he'd come back. And he'd given her children a father figure when he should have been looking for a woman who would give him is own children. But no. He'd loved hers as his own. And he'd loved her unconditionally, even way back when she'd freaked over their age difference.

In ways she'd never understand, they were meant to be in the same story, to have the happy ending they both longed for.

"I'll marry you, Liam," she said softly.

His hands tightened against hers. "Say it again."

Cora wrapped her arms around his neck and brought her lips to his. "Yes," she whispered.

Looking into his beautiful face, his playful, evergreen eyes, his perfect smile that always made him look like he was thinking something naughty, and his cowboy swagger, Cora knew he was it. She'd made a lot of mistakes in her life, but Liam wasn't one of them.

"Are you sure you want us?" she asked, thinking of all the hardships they were sure to face.

"Always," he drawled with a knowing smile, wrapping his arms around her. It was like she never left.

"I love you, Liam." She took a moment to study his face again, clear of confusion and doubt, basking in the moment.

Liam's mouth crushed against hers in celebration. He picked her up and spun her around until her head was as light as her heart.

He fumbled in his pocket and pulled out a ring, clearly vintage with its intricacies.

"It was my grandmother's," he explained. "I've had it since the night we had the fight. I kept hoping..."

Cora felt the need to explain. "It was easier to say goodbye my way than let you break my heart your way."

Liam's mouth quirked up on one side. "How'd that work out for you?"

"Not so well, I'm discovering. I'm sorry."

His deep chuckle soothed her. Pulling her close, Liam buried his nose in her hair, inhaling deeply. She memorized how he felt against her, just like this. Happiness and a calm she'd never experienced settled over her.

She was finally home.

Epilogue

*Being someone's first love may be great, but
to be their last is beyond perfect...*

AFTER GIVING CORA a lingering kiss, thanking her for
breakfast, he took his plate to the sink and stood in the
kitchen for a minute, taking time to appreciate the little
things. He moved to kiss Jolie on the head, as well as
Ashton and Aldin and told them to have a good day.
Their swift hugs caused him to close his eyes and grin. It
was the ordinary time of their days together that made
things extraordinary. He would never take it for granted.
Cora had been through too much—those kids had been
through too much for him to ever become complacent
about anything in his life.

Liam's dad had loved his mother well. He hadn't
been raised in a broken home. He knew what it took for a
man to keep his woman. He knew the hard work it took
to stay happy, and it was a price Liam was more than
willing to pay to keep Cora and their amazing children at
his side. She was still skittish, even with his ring on her
finger and his last name. He supposed it was part of
living a lie with Sam for so long, but he was so happy

she'd found him worth taking a risk. To walk out of her comfort zone and attempt to move on.

He remembered the early days when he'd tried to make her blush with double entendrés and push her with their fiery chemistry. They'd had fun together, but it wasn't until he'd broken down her barriers and lowered his own and they let each other in that their relationship went to the next level. Chemistry would only go so far. He'd spent the next year of their lives proving to her how their age didn't matter and showing her how happy she made him. She'd shown him too, in different ways. She'd been hurt so she needed it spelled out, but he knew she cared when she let him around her kids, kissed him in front of them, asked him to weigh in on a family decision. Those were the moments he lived for. The moments he never knew would define him as a man.

Turns out, Liam hadn't needed some grandiose plan to win Cora back; he'd needed patience and to exhibit his love through actions, not just words. Sam, even in his death, had given Liam one last chance to make it right with Cora. She'd needed to know his love was unconditional. He'd learned a lot about love from Cora. Selfless, patient, long suffering, respect…even after all Sam had put her through, Cora had treated him respectfully and showed her kids how to love someone who wasn't always loveable. How lucky Liam was to be the subject of her adoration now.

Liam stepped out into the early morning air. Behind him, the wife of his dreams, the only woman who could complete him was still fussing over breakfast dishes and the kids were giggling over something inane before the bus picked them up. There was an ethereal fog hovering over the pasture, giving the early fall morning a dream-like feel.

He closed his eyes and sighed, more content than he'd ever thought possible.

The Good Lord shone his blessings differently for everyone in different ways, and in that very moment, Liam had never felt so close. He was thankful for the little things in life that brought back the biggest memories.

And it was times like these, when Liam felt at one with the angels from his past, the light shone a little brighter on their future.

About the Author

Stephanie Taylor is a homeschooling mom of three by day and a writer and business owner by night. She has a doctorate in Multitasking and can actually walk a tight rope while preparing dinner with one hand and typing her next novel with the other. You can find her online on Facebook and Twitter or at her publishing company, Clean Reads. www.cleanreads.com.

Clean Reads
ALL STORY. NO GUILT.

www.ingramcontent.com/pod-product-compliance
Lightning Source LLC
Chambersburg PA
CBHW030418120726

47904CB00007B/2330